ATTACK OF THE ROBBER BEES

Attack of the Robber Bees

Abie Longstaff

Illustrated by

Pablo Gallego

Collins

Contents

Chapter 1

Bea the bee was so excited, she hummed and buzzed in class.

"Bea!" said her teacher. "Stop wriggling."

But Bea couldn't stop, because today she was 20 days old, and she was about to have the best experience of her life. In a few moments, Bea's whole class was going out in a swarm for the first time. They were going to look for pollen and nectar.

Bea had practised her skills. She'd learnt her flowers. She knew which flowers gave the sweetest nectar, and which were bad for bees. She'd learnt her scents.

Flowers

Good: lavender ✓
sweet pea ✓

Not worth the work:
azalea ✗

Scents

Nice: nectar ✓
pollen ✓

Dangerous: pesticide ✗

Most of all, she'd learnt her waggle dance. The waggle was like a kind of map. Whoever found the best flowers came back to the hive and did the waggle dance. The dance showed the worker bees where the flowers were. Then they could go and get the nectar and pollen. Doing the waggle was a serious honour. Bea's big sister, Hannie, had won an award for her waggle technique, and Bea wanted to be just as good.

She pictured the routine. In her mind, she spun in perfect rhythm.

Left spin. Right spin.

Straight. Straight.

SHAKE.

Everyone cheered: "Hooray for Bea! She's a total genius!"

Then the queen would reward HER too, and she'd have a plaque like Hannie. *Yes,* Bea thought. *That's exactly what's going to happen today.*

"Bea!" spluttered her teacher. "Pay attention!"

Everyone was lining up solemnly at the edge of the chamber. She rushed to take her place.

The class wriggled through the interior chambers of the hive, heading towards the exit. Each chamber was a hexagon shape, with six sides made of beige wax. Bea touched the warm wax with her wing. She remembered building this wall, when she was only 12 days old. The junior class had chewed the wax till it was soft, then they'd passed it down in a long chain of bees. Good wax walls helped protect the hive from bacteria.

Bea looked at the bit she had made. There was a little bump on the ceiling where she hadn't smoothed the material properly. She tapped it now with her foot, to smooth it down. Oops! Now she'd made it too thin. That wasn't safe. *I'll come back and fix it later,* thought Bea to herself.

Bea wiggled past the nursery chambers, waving to Mum. Mum was a nurse bee. She looked after the eggs the queen laid and fed pollen to the newborn bees, just as she had done for Bea.

A rush of fresh air hit Bea. They were nearly at the exit! She trembled with exhilaration. Up ahead, bees were already leaving the hive.

Bea hopped from foot to foot. Her wings quivered and her abdomen fizzed inside. She grinned at a bee guard, standing just by the exit. The guard nodded at her sternly and went back to watching for enemies and predators.

The bee in front of Bea took off. Now it was Bea's turn! She stepped to the edge. The hive was high up in an old tree. Very, very high. A whirr of fear rushed up from Bea's feet. She took a deep breath. *I can do this*, she told herself. She sniffed the breeze. There was the barest hint of lavender coming from the east! She scanned the area.

"Hi Bea!" warbled a voice. Bea spun round. Hannie was there! Bea smiled at her sister.

"Are you here to see me off?" she said, proudly.

"No, silly, I'm coming with you," said Hannie. "Senior class are going to guide you today. Leaving the hive can be scary for *juniors*. But it's easy for us *seniors*," she added, breezily.

Bea looked down. She wanted to do this by herself. And now Hannie was here, so Bea had zero chance of impressing anyone.

Bonus

Parts of a bee

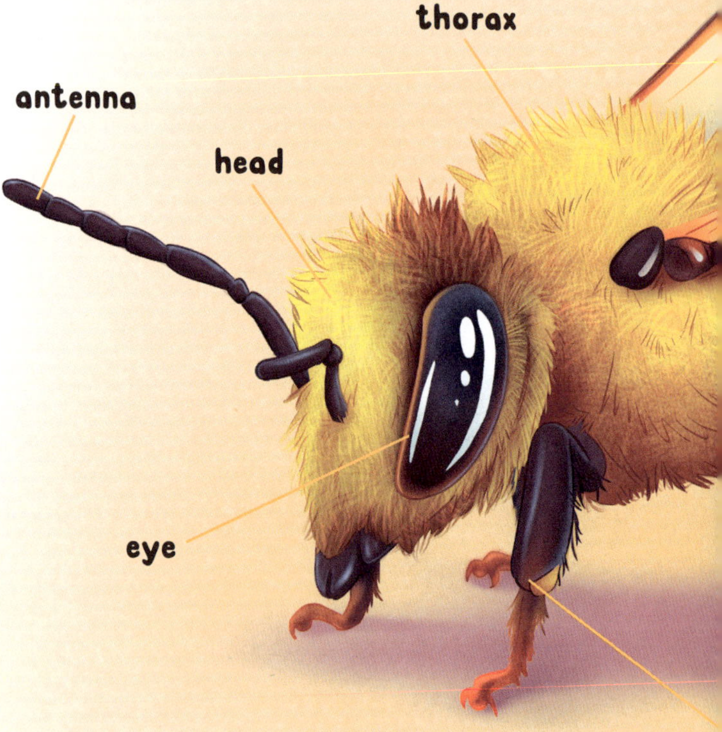

wings
abdomen
stinger
pollen basket
legs

Chapter 2

"Go, Bea!" buzzed her teacher.

Bea tensed her wings and soared out of the hive. She breathed in the smells of flowers and grass. As she flew, she kicked her legs in joy. This scouting trip was brilliant! Not even Hannie being here could sabotage it.

"Stick with me, Bea," said Hannie. "We can only stay out for an hour and I want to collect as much nectar as possible. Bea? Are you listening?"

Bea was listening in a vague way, while secretly working out ways to persuade Hannie to buzz off and leave her alone.

"I can do this myself," said Bea. "Honest. I know we have two stomachs, one for storing nectar. I know how to collect pollen on my back legs. I even know how to do the waggle dance. I don't need a companion."

“But I’m in the seniors,” said Hannie. “I’ll make sure you do everything PERFECTLY.”

Bea breathed deeply, focusing on the land below her. It was a bright array of colours – reds and yellows and greens and – oh! There was the lavender she had smelt. Its soft purple strands waved in the wind.

She glanced sideways at Hannie. Her sister was flying on. She hadn't spotted the plant. But Bea knew lavender guaranteed good nectar. She slowed down, working out the angle of the sun and the way from the hive to the lavender. She quickly turned back to the hive. It wasn't that she wanted to *deceive* Hannie. But if Bea got back to the hive first, she could do the waggle to show everyone how to reach the lavender.

"Bea!" cried Hannie. "Where are you ... oh! ... lavender! I must tell the hive!" She zipped to catch Bea.

"I'll tell them, Hannie!" shouted Bea. She shot at top speed towards home, buzzing through the door of the hive. She couldn't wait to do the waggle!

"Lavender!" she cried. Her eyes slowly adjusted to the darkness of the hive.

"Where?" asked her teacher.

Bea put her foot out to start doing the waggle dance routine – wait, was it left first? Or right? Too late! Hannie was already waggling, turning on the spot to show the direction of the lavender.

"Great waggle, Hannie," said the guard, waving a swarm of workers out of the hive.

"Hannie!" snapped Bea. "You sabotaged my waggle." She was seething inside. Why did Hannie always get to do everything first?

"Bea. You know we have to be fast," said Hannie, "for the good of the hive."

"I was *going* to be fast!" cried Bea. It was so unfair. She'd had her foot out ready to go. A shot of rage welled up in her thorax.

"I was only *helping*," said Hannie.

"I don't need your help, Hannie!" cried Bea. "You ruined my first trip!"

Bea turned angrily and flew out of the hive.

"Bea! Come back!" Hannie shouted.

"Buzz off, Hannie!" yelled Bea. "Leave me alone!"

Bea flew on, past the worker bees on the lavender, and between the sweet peas. She flew through the smell of long grass, over the brook and beyond the meadow. She was so furious her wings just wanted to MOVE. *Buzz, buzz, buzz,* they beat in rhythm, and every beat meant "Buzz off, Hannie."

Bea flew until she couldn't fly any more. She sank onto a sunflower, exhausted.

But there was another bee already on the flower.

"Hello," said Bea. "I'm Bea. I come from the hive in the old tree."

"Oh really?" said the new bee. She turned, showing Bea her stinger. "Now. You are going to tell me exactly how to get to your hive, and how much honey is stored there."

The other bee was a robber bee! The robber bee loomed over Bea. Her eyes looked cold and scary.

Bea shook with fear.

Waggle dance

1 The waggle run: this shows the distance and direction to the flower.

2 The return: a quick return to the start means the food is good.

3 Repeating the waggle run: the more the bee waggles, the better the food is.

4 The return: back to the start of the waggle run again.

Chapter 3

Bea shrank back, warily.

Robber bees were barbarians! They stole honey from hives. This robber was a spy. She was spying for her own swarm, finding out the locations of hives.

"Tell me how to get to your hive," said the robber. Her voice was low and sinister.

Bea's heart was pounding. But there was one thing she was sure of. She wasn't going to tell the robber bee the way to her hive.

The robber waved her stinger. It was covered in tiny, sharp hooks.

Bea tensed her abdomen. She had a stinger too. But she wasn't sure how to use it. They hadn't done that lesson yet.

The robber stepped towards Bea, twitching her stinger.

Bea's body trembled and tiny bits of pollen fell off her legs.

Suddenly, she remembered a lesson they *had* done. Pollen release! A plan slipped into her head. But, for her trick to work, she'd have to time it perfectly. The robber came closer. Swish, swish went her stinger.

Not yet, Bea told herself.

Nearly ...

Nearly ...

The robber was glaring at Bea, with wild eyes.

Now!

Bea rubbed her back legs to release the pollen and ...

Flick!

She tossed the fine powder right into those scary eyes.

"No!" The robber put her front legs up to her eyes, and Bea hurtled off the sunflower, zipping away as fast as she could.

Bea's breath was tight in her throat. Would the robber follow her?

She sped into the woods, ducking under branches and in and out of leaves. She pushed her exhausted body on, forcing her wings to GO … until she could go no further. Her wings stopped in mid-air. There wasn't a single beat left in them.

Bea plummeted …

down …

down …

Flump!

She landed on a foxglove flower.

She was deep in the woods. Her wings were sore. Her body ached. A scary thought hit Bea: *I don't know if I can make it home.*

"At least I didn't tell the robber the way to the hive," mumbled Bea.

Her exhausted body finally relaxed.

"No!" came a cry. A ginger bee landed beside her. "Stay awake!" he begged, aghast.

"T-too tired," stammered Bea.

"Drink this!" He held her head and poured sweet nectar into her mouth.

A rush of sugar energy hit Bea. She blinked. She looked at the other bee, warily.

"I won't hurt you," he promised. "I'm not like that robber bee. I don't have a stinger. My name is Mason."

"I'm Bea." She sat up. "Thank you for giving me nectar. I feel much better now. Is your hive nearby, Mason?"

"No!" Mason laughed. "I don't have a hive," he said. "I'm a solitary bee." He waved his legs airily. "I live by myself. I drink nectar and buzz around."

"But why are you buzzing around here?" Bea frowned.

Mason blushed redder than his ginger fur. "Actually ... well ... I'm looking for love."

"Love?"

"I know my soulmate is out there," said Mason. "I just haven't met her yet. But I will. I've even written poems for her. Do you want to hear one?"

"Sure," said Bea.

Mason spread his front leg out and declared:

"*Your wings are like a summer breeze,*
Let's fly together through the trees.
With every flutter, every flight,
You make my world so pure and bright."

He put his leg back down. "What do you think?" he said.

"Well." Bea wanted to be kind. "At least it rhymes."

"I used a dictionary! I tried to find a rhyme for 'buzz', but I couldn't come up with a good one."

"Does?" suggested Bea. "Fuzz?"

"Ooo, yes!" said Mason. "I'll use that for the next verse. '*I love your soft fuzz.*' Something like that?"

"Good!" said Bea. Mason was such a cool guy. Maybe she could be a solitary bee too? That way she'd get to do everything by herself.

Kinds of bees

Red mason

Solitary bee. They nest in the spaces between bricks.

Garden bumblebee

They live in hives which they line with leaves and animal fur. They collect pollen but do not make honey.

Robber (a kind of honeybee)

When there is
a shortage of nectar
some honey bees
steal from other hives!

Patchwork leaf-cutter

Solitary bee.
They cut up leaves
to make their nests.

Tawny mining bee

Solitary bee.
Mainly seen in spring,
they make nest tunnels
in banks and lawns.

Chapter 4

Bea and Mason spent all morning making up rhymes. Being a solitary bee was fun! You didn't have to collect pollen or nurse baby bees or make wax walls for the hive. In fact, you didn't have a hive at all! Mason explained that he nested in a crack in a tree.

"It sounds great!" exclaimed Bea. Mason was so free. Nobody bossed him around or told him off. He got to do EVERYTHING he wanted.

Bea and Mason buzzed from flower to flower, darting onto a daisy and finally landing on a thistle flower.

"I'm thinking of taking up the guitar," said Mason. "I might have more chance with my soulmate if I could sing my poems."

Bea was struggling with a bit of dust on the base of her wing. She wriggled and twisted but she couldn't reach it. *Mason can get it,* she said to herself, and she began the grooming dance, stamping her legs and twisting her back.

"What are you doing?" Mason laughed. "Hahaha. That's hilarious!"

"I'm telling you to get this bit of dust off me," said Bea. "In the hive, we do this exact dance, and bees come rushing to clean us."

"Really?" said Mason.

"Yes. And if you move your head like this – " she showed him, "you get a little massage too."

"Wow!" said Mason. "Being in a hive sounds fun."

"Sharing IS fun!" said Bea. "We all work so hard together but we play together too. When a new queen comes, we all do a big dance of joy."

"When I find my queen, I guess I'll have to do that dance by myself," said Mason. He twisted his head. "Are you missing your hive, Bea?"

All at once a pang of loneliness hit Bea. She pictured the hive, warm and dark. She'd helped make the walls, the ceilings. She'd swept every corridor to keep it clean. It was home. It was where her friends were, where her family lived.

Her eyes filled with tears.

"Yes, I'm homesick," she said. The hive was what mattered. She remembered the moment Hannie had got to do the waggle.

"You know we have to be *fast*," Hannie had said, "*for the good of the hive*."

A rush of guilt filled Bea. Hannie was right. It might be annoying that Hannie had got there first *again*, but Bea had hesitated. And that was not good for the hive.

Bea put her head in her front legs.

"I shouted at my sister," she confessed. "I told her to buzz off." Tears streamed down her face. "But I miss her. I really do."

Mason patted her shoulder.

"I messed up my first scouting trip," said Bea. "I flew away from the swarm. I'm so ashamed. I can't face anyone! I can't ever go home."

"That sounds really hard," said Mason. "But Bea ... you escaped a robber bee! You're brave and clever."

Bea sniffed. "I don't feel so clever."

"Your family will think you are," said Mason.

Bea nodded slowly. "Mum will be worried," she said.

"I'm sure she loves you," said Mason. "Your sister does too."

"But how can I go back?" howled Bea. "What will I say?"

"You'll say – " Mason cleared his throat. He spread out his front leg. "SORRY!"

"That's all?" asked Bea.

"Yes," said Mason. "I was trying to make it rhyme but I couldn't think of a word. 'Lorry'? No. But the thing is, Bea, that one word is powerful enough on its own."

"Do you really think so?" said Bea.

"I know it," said Mason.

Bea wiped her eyes. She could do that! She could say sorry.

She looked around. She was deep in the forest. A cold rush of panic hit her.

"Mason!" she cried, in anguish. "I don't know the way home!"

Bonus

Bee jokes

What goes zzub-zzub?
A bee flying backwards.
What do you call a bee that can't decide?
A may-bee.
What is black and yellow and buzzes along the bottom of the sea?
A bee in a submarine.
What do you do with a sick wasp?
Take it to waspital.
What bee keeps you healthy?
Vitamin bee.

Chapter 5

Bea spun around on the thistle, in confusion. Was home towards the east? The west?

"I can't remember!" Bea cried.

"You must have a map on you, or a guidebook?" asked Mason.

"No, no," said Bea. "Honey bees don't have any maps because we learn our way as we go."

"Let's try remembering, then," said Mason, calmly. "Where were we before this thistle?"

Bea thought hard. She'd practised remembering in class. *I can do this*, she told herself. A vague picture came into her head.

"Before the thistle was ... a daisy!" she cried. "A bright white one!"

"Good!" said Mason. They flew up from the thistle towards the daisy. "And when I found you, you were on a foxglove – "

"That's over in this area," said Bea. The woods were growing lighter. The afternoon sun peeped through the leaves. "This is the way out of the woods – " said Bea, as they darted from flower to flower, "because here's the sunflower where I saw the robber bee."

"You're doing brilliantly, Bea."

"Now I know where to go!" said Bea. "It's the brook and then the long grass, the sweet peas and the lavender and ... Mason?"

Mason was staring off to the side.

"Mason?" Bea repeated.

"Hang on," he said. "I hear a soft buzzing. What a beautiful voice! Have you ever heard such warm, gentle humming?"

A ginger bee popped up from a yellow petal.

“Mmm,” said Mason, dreamily. “She smells like roses and rain.”

Bea nudged him. “Mason,” she said, “I think you might have found your soulmate!”

Mason turned to Bea. “How do I look?” he asked, seriously. “Is my fur neat?”

“You look great,” whispered Bea. “Now seize the moment. Go talk to her!”

“I can’t remember my poem!” Mason gasped.

"You can," said Bea. "*Your wings are like a summer breeze –* "

"And hers really ARE!"

"Good luck," said Bea. "Thank you for everything."

"Good luck to you too, Bea. I hope you get home soon."

Bea hid behind a sunflower and smiled to herself as she watched Mason make a new friend. Then she turned and flew into the meadow, over the brook and through the long grass. Before long, she passed the sweet peas and then the lavender. She rested for a moment on various flowers, topping up on nectar and pollen.

Her hive was in sight now, up high in the old tree. All she had to do was fly in, find Hannie, and say sorry.

Bea nodded to herself. She was ready. And she had so many adventures to tell. She'd been away for hours! She looked back to see how far she'd come.

There was a dark shadow in the distance, like a beige cloud. The air was filled with a loud hum. Bea squinted. A swarm of bees was coming. That wasn't HER swarm. She froze in horror as she recognised one bee right at the front. The robber! Bea had told her the hive was in an old tree and the robbers had found it. They were coming to attack!

It's my fault! thought Bea, aghast. The robbers would take all their honey!

She shot up from the lavender, whizzing towards the hive at full speed.

"Bea?" said the guard at the entrance.

"Robbers!" cried Bea. "Raise the alarm!"

The guard waved the tip of her abdomen, and a perfume filled the air. The smell spread through the hive, so everyone knew there was danger.

Bees came rushing from every chamber towards the hive exit.

"Get back, Bea!" yelled the guard. "Hide where it's safe."

But Bea shook her head. This was HER fault. If she hadn't left, or flown so far, she would never have met the ghastly robber bee and alerted her to this hive. She felt so guilty.

"I'm going to fight," cried Bea, "for the good of the hive!"

Bonus

Map of the hive

Honey is stored at the top of the hive.

Nursery chambers: nurse bees feed the baby bees pollen, honey and royal jelly.

Royal jelly is stored here. It is used to feed the queen and baby bees.

Guard bees keep the hive safe.

Pollen is taken into the hive and stored.

The bees make wax which they chew and shape.

H_2O

Chapter 6

"Here come the robbers!" cried the guard. "Protect the hive!"

Bea flicked her stinger up ready.

There was a whirring and humming, and the air was filled with robber bees. It was war!

Whack!

Whump!

The guards shoved the invading swarm away from the hive.

Bea's teacher grabbed her. "We have to surround the robbers and trap them," she said.

Together the class circled the robber bees and moved in tighter. They squished the robber bees into a huddle.

"Now heat your bodies!" yelled the teacher. Bea buzzed, shaking her body to raise her temperature. The group of bees grew hotter and hotter until the robber bees couldn't bear it. They sank to the ground.

"Hooray!" cried Bea. But more robbers were coming. *There are too many!* thought Bea, in anguish. *We can't fight all these barbarians!*

A series of robber bees entered the hive, shoving the guards aside.

"My home!" cried Bea. It was lost. It was all lost.

"You again!" snapped a furious voice. It was the robber bee from the sunflower. "You escaped once, but I won't let you go this time." She pointed her stinger at Bea.

Bea fell to her knees. Now she'd never get to tell Hannie she loved her. "I'm sorry, Hannie," she whispered.

"Tell me where you keep the honey," said the robber.

Bea paused, staring at the waxy floor. There was that bumpy bit that needed smoothing. Suddenly, it gave her an idea. She could deceive the robbers!

"I'll show you," she said. She pushed to the exit. "It's quicker to go from the outside." Bea buzzed into the air and led the way to the back of the hive.

Please let me have remembered this right, she thought. She needed to find the place where the ceiling was weak. She'd have to guess. Guess AND be lucky.

"Our honey is through there," said Bea. "If you push your way in, you'll have it all."

The robber bees shoved the outer walls of the hive, biting the wax to make an entrance.

Bea buzzed back to the front of the hive and dashed inside. She hurried along the corridors she knew so well, twisting in and out and up. Soon she was on the floor above the robber bees.

"Everyone!" called Bea. "Help me stamp!"

"Bea?" said a voice. It was Hannie. "What are you doing?"

"Trust me, Hannie. I know what to do."

Hannie looked into her eyes. "I trust you, Bea," she said, solemnly, and she began to stamp. All the bees jumped together with a steady rhythm.

Bang ...

bang ...

bang ... until ...

Flump!

The floor fell away, onto the robber bees!

The hive bees hovered in the air as the robbers were covered in heavy wax.

"Take that!" yelled the guard. "Get out of our hive."

The robber bees buzzed furiously away.

"You did it, Bea!" cried Hannie.

Bea's legs were weak. She sank down onto the mess of wax.

"Hannie, I'm sorry I yelled at you," she said.

"I'm sorry too," said Hannie. "I bossed you about too much. I see how clever and daring you are now. You can take care of yourself."

Bea grinned. She told Hannie about meeting the robber bee, and all about Mason.

"You've had such an adventure!" said Hannie, in amazement.

Just then there was a hum of excitement. Out came the queen!

"Where is the junior bee who saved us?" she asked.

Hannie pushed Bea forward. "It was my brilliant sister, Bea," she said, proudly.

Bea's mouth opened and closed. She didn't know what to say.

"Thank you," said the queen. "In all my reign, I've never seen such a brave bee. Because of you, we are victorious."

"Hooray for Bea!" everyone cried. "She's a total genius."

Bea grinned. She'd always known the day would turn out exactly like this.

How bees make honey

1. Bees collect nectar from flowers, sucking it into a honey sac or second stomach.

2. Bees return to the hive and chew on the nectar, passing it from bee to bee. This turns the nectar into honey.

3. They store the honey in honeycomb cells.

4. The bees flap their wings over the honey, to evaporate the water. This thickens the honey. They then seal the cells with fresh wax.

About the author

What do you enjoy about writing?

I love going into different worlds. Sometimes I invent my own worlds and make up all kinds of creatures. Sometimes, like in this story, I pretend I'm a completely different creature, which is fun.

Abie Longstaff

Why did you decide to write this story?

Because, generally, I think rules are important. We all have to work together and get on ... but it's not always easy to follow other people's rules. Sometimes we all want to do something for ourselves that breaks the rules a bit. In this story, I wanted to look at that. Bees were the perfect characters to choose because their life is based on following rules.

Did you use any real-life experiences to shape the story?

I'm a big sister myself and I always got to do everything first. That must have been very annoying for my younger sisters. Sometimes I wanted to be alone and not have to look after my younger sisters. I tried to get both of those feelings into this story.

What did you enjoy most about writing this book?

For Bea's story, I got to pretend that I was a bee. I love drawing maps. I often start stories by doodling a map and seeing what world I invent. So, it was great to draw the map of Bea's hive and of the meadow she flies over.

Did you have to research the story? Did you find out anything that surprised you?

I had to look up lots of facts about bees, such as how they deal with predators. I didn't know there were so many different kinds of bees, and I certainly didn't know that bees have five eyes!

Which character do you think you are most like? Why?

I'm probably most like Bea's big sister Hannie. I can be a bit too bossy sometimes.

How do you feel when readers enjoy your books?

I love getting messages from parents to say a child has enjoyed my books. I also like going into schools and making up stories with children. Reading and writing for pleasure are really important. Reading makes us happy!

What do you hope readers will get from this book?

I hope children will enjoy learning about bees. If you find bees as interesting as I do, you can look for books about bees in your library.

About the illustrator

Pablo Gallego

What made you want to be an illustrator?

I always liked to draw from a very young age. I spent hours drawing. And I really liked watching cartoons.

How did you start illustrating?

I was always very curious, wanting to learn more and more, studying and practising by myself. Along the way I met many colleagues who helped me in my growth and learning as an illustrator.

What was the best thing about illustrating this book?

In all the books I have worked on, I enjoy the creative process that is awakened with each new story. And I enjoy each page as if it were a unique piece of art. I try to convey what happens on that page, so that all the action can be understood just by looking at the image.

What was the most difficult scene to illustrate?

I think that the first scenes are always the most difficult. It's easier when one becomes familiar with the characters and the story.

How do you bring characters to life?

It's a process that takes some time. I do a lot of tests, and until I'm happy with the character I don't consider it finished. The character has to convey the same personality throughout the story. And I also like to work on the secondary characters that appear less often, as well as the settings. I'm trying to create all the elements needed to tell the entire story, and make the story world come alive.

Did you have to do a lot of research on bees?

I always like to research the subject in each new project. That helps me get even more into the story.

What materials do you use to illustrate?

I work with a graphic tablet.

Is there anything in this book that relates to your own experiences?

Finding a creative solution to the unforeseen problems that arise in life! That's what Bea does at the end of the book, to save the hive.

Did you learn anything about bees while illustrating this book?

Yes! I never imagined the variety of bees that exist. I knew a little about how bees work and organise themselves, but I didn't know about all the different kinds of bee.

Book chat

Which part of the book did you like best?

Which of the bee characters are you most like and why?

Do any of the characters change through the story?

What do you think Bea learned from her adventure?

If you could ask the author anything, what would you ask?

What kind of bee would you like to be and why?

Who would you recommend this book to and why?

Are any parts of the story sad or frustrating?

Do you like the title of the book? Why or why not?

Book challenge:

Hide something from a friend. Perform your own waggle dance to lead them to it.

Collins
BIG CAT

Published by Collins
An imprint of HarperCollins*Publishers*

The News Building
1 London Bridge Street
London SE1 9GF
UK

Macken House
39/40 Mayor Street Upper
Dublin 1
D01 C9W8
Ireland

10 9 8 7 6 5 4 3 2 1

ISBN 978-0-00-874634-6

British Library Cataloguing-in-Publication Data
A catalogue record for this publication is available from the British Library.

Download the teaching notes and word cards to accompany this book at:
http://littlewandle.org.uk/signupfluency/

Author: Abie Longstaff
Illustrator: Pablo Gallego (Beehive Illustration)
Colourist: Ilias Arahovitis (Beehive Illustration)
Publisher: Laura White
Product managers: Caroline Green and Holly Woolnough
Series editor: Charlotte Raby
Commissioning editor: Caroline Green
Phonics consultant: Catherine Baker
Project manager: Emily Hooton
Copyeditor: Sally Byford
Proofreader: Catherine Dakin
Cover designer: Sarah Finan
Typesetter: 2Hoots Publishing Services Ltd
Production controller: Katharine Willard

Printed in the UK.

FSC www.fsc.org MIX Paper | Supporting responsible forestry FSC™ C007454

This book contains FSC™ certified paper and other controlled sources to ensure responsible forest management.

For more information visit: www.harpercollins.co.uk/green

Made with responsibly sourced paper and vegetable ink

Scan to see how we are reducing our environmental impact.